Happy Birthday
Lily!
♡ Love,
Aaron, Molly, Eli
& Sequoia
2013

Kathleen Hague

Illustrated by Michael Hague

Good Night, Fairies

SeaStar Books * New York

To Devon

SEASTAR BOOKS
A division of NORTH-SOUTH BOOKS INC.

First published in the United States by SeaStar Books, a division of North-South Books Inc., New York.
Published simultaneously in Great Britain, Canada, Australia, and New Zealand by North-South Books,
an imprint of Nord-Süd Verlag AG, Gossau Zürich, Switzerland.

Library of Congress Cataloging-in-Publication Data
Hague, Kathleen.
Good night, fairies / by Kathleen Hague; illustrated by Michael Hague.
p. cm.
Summary: At bedtime, a mother tells her curious child about the things that fairies do,
like hang the stars in the evening sky and care for the toys that children have lost.
[1. Fairies—Fiction. 2. Bedtime—Fiction. 3. Mother and child—Fiction.]
I. Hague, Michael, ill. II. Title.
PZ7.H1246 Go 2002   [E]—dc21   2001049867

The artwork for this book was prepared by using pen and ink, watercolor, and colored pencils.
Book design by Nicole Stanco de las Heras.

ISBN 1-58717-134-1 (reinforced trade edition)
3 5 7 9 RTE 10 8 6 4 2

Printed in Hong Kong

For more information about our books, and the authors and artists who create them, visit our web site: www.northsouth.com

"It's time for bed," said Mother.

"I was wondering," said the child.

"About what?" asked Mother.

"About fairies."

"Hop into bed," said Mother as she turned off the light.

"and I'll tell you what I know about fairies."

"What do the fairies do when it's nighttime?"
asked the child.

"Well, the fairies hang the stars in the evening sky,"
answered Mother, "so every child will have

a night-light."

"Why?" asked the child.

"Because fairies love little children like you,"
said Mother. "Of all the world's creatures,
there is nothing so like a fairy as a child."
"Do fairies have toys?" asked the child.
"Fairies don't have toys of their own, but they gather
and care for all of the toys children have lost,"
answered Mother.

"Do fairies ever sleep?" asked the child.
"On leafy beds in secret gardens," said Mother.

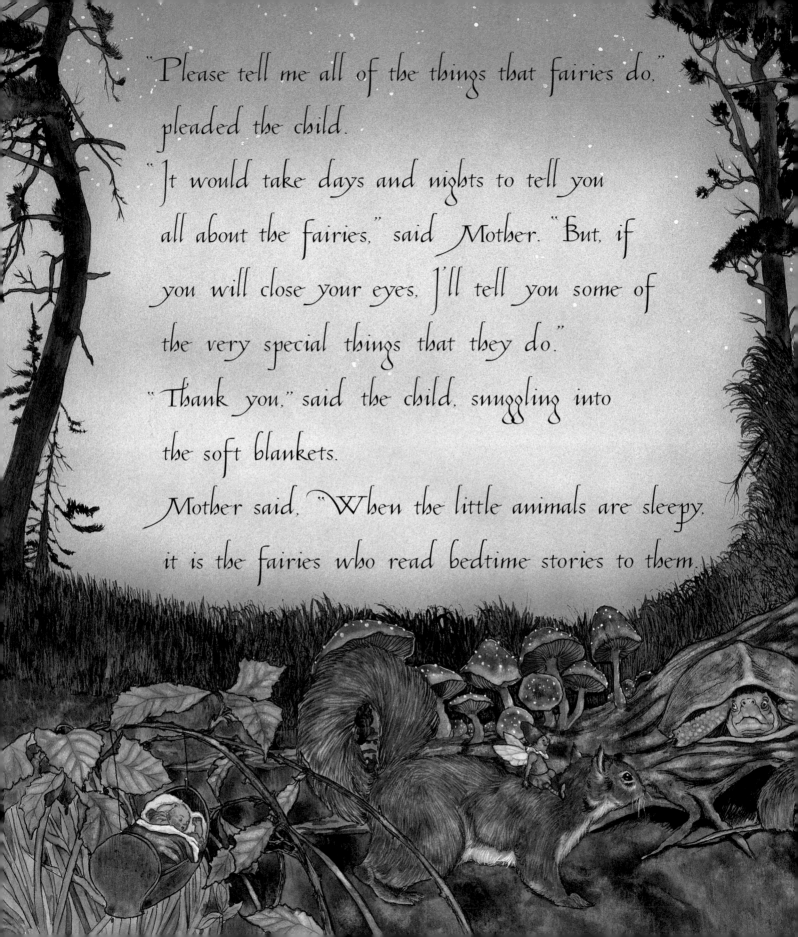

"Please tell me all of the things that fairies do," pleaded the child.

"It would take days and nights to tell you all about the fairies," said Mother. "But, if you will close your eyes, I'll tell you some of the very special things that they do."

"Thank you," said the child, snuggling into the soft blankets.

Mother said, "When the little animals are sleepy, it is the fairies who read bedtime stories to them.

Other fairies paint the wings of tiny bugs
and make the butterflies beautiful.

There are fairies who teach the birds to sing . . .

...and the unicorns to fly.

It is the fairies who comb the mermaids' hair . . .

...and draw rainbows to brighten rainy days.

It is the fairies who scatter the autumn leaves

and paint the winter world white.

Fairies make the spring flowers bloom.

And on warm summer nights they dress in
spiders' lace and dance to the twilight orchestra.

And when little ones close their eyes and go to sleep,
it is the fairies who welcome them to dreamland."

"Good night," whispered Mother. But the child was already far, far away.

Can you find and count all 321 winged fairies in this book?
Don't forget to look at the endpapers!